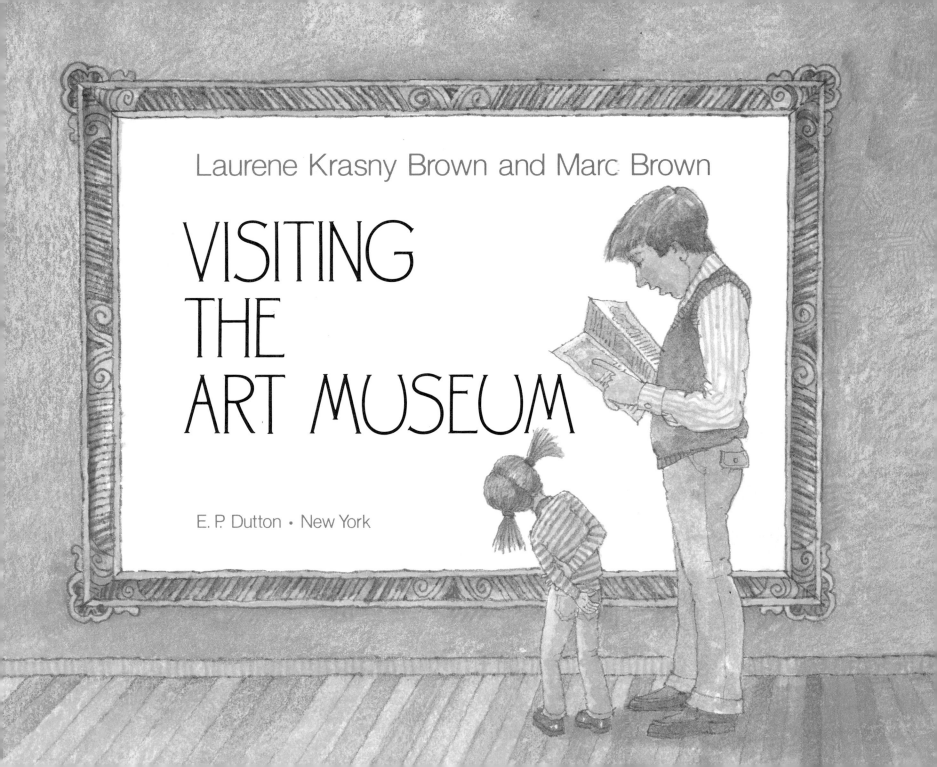

Laurene Krasny Brown and Marc Brown

VISITING THE ART MUSEUM

E. P. Dutton • New York

Cover art credits are on page 32.

Copyright © 1986 by Laurene Krasny Brown and Marc Brown
All rights reserved.

Library of Congress Cataloging in Publication Data

Brown, Laurene Krasny.
   Visiting the art museum.

   Summary: As a family wanders through an art museum, they see
examples of various art styles from primitive through twentieth-century pop art.
   1. Art museums—Visitors—United States—Juvenile literature.
2. Art appreciation—Juvenile literature.   [1. Art museums.   2. Museums.
3. Art appreciation]   I. Brown, Marc Tolon.   II. Title.
N510.B76   1986   708.13   85-32552   ISBN 0-525-44233-2

Published in the United States by E. P. Dutton, 2 Park Avenue, New York, N.Y. 10016

Published simultaneously in Canada by Fitzhenry & Whiteside Limited, Toronto

Editor: Ann Durell   Designer: Isabel Warren-Lynch

Printed in Hong Kong by South China Printing Co.
First Edition   COBE   10 9 8 7 6 5 4 3 2 1

3

4

5

NO, PEOPLE MAKE COSTUMES TO WEAR OTHER TIMES TOO. THIS ONE WAS WORN FOR A CEREMONY THE ASMAT HAD WHEN SOMEBODY DIED.

IT'S JUST SOME STRAW AND FEATHERS AND OTHER JUNK. WHAT'S SO SCARY?

THIS IS SCARY. IS IT FOR HALLOWEEN?

9

SINCE ARMOR COVERED A MAN'S WHOLE BODY, THE ONLY WAY PEOPLE COULD TELL WHO WAS INSIDE WAS BY THE COAT OF ARMS ON HIS SHIELD.

SWORD · WESTERN EUROPEAN · 1400

PARADE RAPIER · GERMAN · 1606

The Metropolitan Museum of Art.
Gift of William H. Riggs, 1913, and Fletcher Fund, 1939.
Copyright © 1986 by The Metropolitan Museum of Art.

LOOK AT THE TEETH ON THIS SHARK! THAT MAN WILL LOSE MORE THAN HIS CLOTHES.

DON'T FEEL BAD, ROSIE. THE MAN OVERBOARD WAS SAVED. HE LIVED TO BECOME LORD MAYOR OF LONDON.

IT'S A MEAN PICTURE. I HATE IT!

Auguste Renoir
Two Little Circus Girls,
Oil on canvas, 1879, 51½ x 38½"
Potter Palmer Collection 22.440
© The Art Institute of Chicago. All Rights Reserved.

18

19

Rousseau, Henri.
The Sleeping Gypsy. 1897.
Oil on canvas, 51" x 6'7".
Collection, The Museum of Modern Art, New York.
Gift of Mrs. Simon Guggenheim.

MOMMY, LOOK AT THIS LION. HE WHISPERS, "WATCH OUT OR I'LL EAT YOU UP!" BUT SHE DOESN'T HEAR HIM.

BECAUSE SHE'S SLEEPING. WHAT DO YOU THINK SHE IS DREAMING ABOUT?

THIS WAS PAINTED BY HENRI ROUSSEAU. HE NEVER STUDIED ART. HE TAUGHT HIMSELF TO PAINT.

MAYBE THERE'S HOPE FOR ME.

20

21

Pollock, Jackson (American, 1912–1956)
Portrait and a Dream
1953
PAINTING enamel on canvas
H 58⅛" x W 134¼"
1967.8
Dallas Museum of Art, gift of Mr. and Mrs. Algur H. Meadows and the Meadows Foundation Incorporated

23

26

MORE ABOUT THE ART

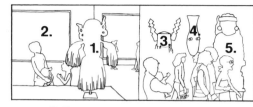

pages 6-7

PRIMITIVE GALLERY

The word *primitive* refers to the art of those people who, over the years, have done their work using tools but no modern machines. Primitive artists have no formal schooling in art. People in countries all over the world have made primitive art.

1. This costume was constructed in the 1900s by the Asmat people of Irian Jaya, New Guinea. To make it, they used natural materials such as palm leaves, rattan, seeds, feathers, and wood.

2. Based on a painting of crocodiles and wallabies, made on tree bark by the Banjo of Umba Kumba, Australia

3. Based on a Katchina mask painted on leather by Zuni Indians of southwest America

4. Based on a mask carved from wood by the Grebo, a seagoing tribe of Ivory Coast, Africa

5. Based on a stone warrior made by the Toltecs of Mexico

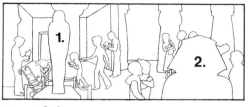

pages 8-9

ANCIENT EGYPTIAN GALLERY

Even though its culture ended almost two thousand years ago, a lot is known about life in ancient Egypt. One reason is that the Egyptians preserved in their tombs many possessions which they expected to use in their life after death. The Egyptians also took great care with burying people.

1. This mummy case was made to hold the body of a woman named Tabes. She was the singer at the Temple of Amun, and her husband was the barber there. Her mummy must still be inside, because the case has not been opened since it was sealed in about 940 B.C.

2. Based on a sculpture of Pharaoh Thutmose III. During his reign, Thutmose conquered many foreign neighbors and added their lands to Egypt's empire.

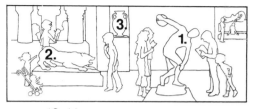

pages 10-11

CLASSICAL GREEK AND ROMAN GALLERY

Greek artists were the first to make sculptures of people and animals that looked almost as natural as living beings. The Greeks studied the body's structure, or anatomy, to learn where the muscles and bones were and how they worked.

1. This marble *Discus Thrower* is a Roman copy of a Greek statue made in about 450 B.C. Discus throwing was one event at early Olympic Games, along with chariot races, boxing, and many other sports. But at the first Olympics, there was only one event, a running race. The length of this race, 630 feet, is said to have been the distance Hercules could walk while holding his breath.

2. Based on a Greek sculpture made in the 400s B.C.

3. Based on a vase painted by Psiax, a Greek artist, in about 525 B.C. The picture shows Hercules strangling the Nemean lion.

pages 12–13

ARMS AND ARMOR GALLERY

Warriors in the 500s to 1500s wore armor to protect their bodies during battle. The knight was a warrior with enough money to own a horse and enough means to keep his followers well cared for and safe.

1. This man's battle armor was made by French metalworkers in about 1550. The horse's armor is from Italy. A knight on horseback, wearing armor like this, would carry a long lance, a sword, and a steel club or mace. Then in the 1600s, pistols became popular and began to replace both armor and lances.

2. Based on parade armor made for the French king Henry II. It might take a skilled metalworker two years to fashion armor as fancy as this.

3. Based on Italian armor made in about 1400. The sleeveless jacket is soft velvet on the outside, but it has steel plates on the inside.

pages 14–15

RENAISSANCE GALLERY

The word *renaissance* means rebirth in French. Between the 1300s and 1500s, artists realized they could learn a lot by looking back in history to classical Greek and Roman times. For example, Renaissance artists revived the practice of showing people and other living things in a realistic way.

1. This painting, *The Battle of San Romano,* by Paolo di Dono (known as Uccello) tells about an actual battle fought between Florentines and Sienese in Italy in 1432. The Florentine captain is the man in the center riding a white horse. By the way, his side won.

2. Based on a painting, *Saint George and the Dragon,* by Raffaello Sanzio (known as Raphael), dated 1504–05. Saint George is said to have killed dragons in England, Germany, and even Africa.

3. Based on the sculptor Donatello's statue of *Saint George,* made from 1415 to 1417.

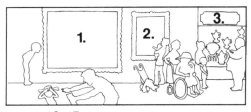

pages 16–17

EIGHTEENTH CENTURY GALLERY

Since cameras were not yet invented by the 1700s, paintings and drawings were the only way to record people, places, and events. Artists made paintings about all sorts of subjects: splendid things, tragic things, and also everyday things.

1. This 1778 painting, *Watson and the Shark,* by John Singleton Copley, re-creates an accident—when Brook Watson fell overboard in the harbor at Havana, Cuba. He was rescued, but he did lose a leg to the shark. Copley made three different paintings of this scene.

2. Based on a portrait of a Spanish count's son, painted by Francisco Goya in 1787. Goya was the official painter of the king of Spain.

3. Paul Revere, the famous American patriot and silversmith, made all his pieces by hand, carefully hammering the silver into shapes of teapots, mugs, and other useful things.

pages 18–19

IMPRESSIONIST GALLERY

According to a group of French artists working in the 1870s, artists should depict the world as they see it, using whatever style they want. Many of these Impressionist artists chose to paint or sculpt subjects from circuses, dance halls, and other places of entertainment.

1. Pierre-Auguste Renoir painted this picture, *Two Little Circus Girls,* in 1879. He liked to show people in their own surroundings, doing what they usually did, not posed and stiff in the artist's studio. Renoir got his first job when he was thirteen years old, painting designs on porcelain plates.

2. Based on a painting, *The Bath,* done in 1891 by Mary Cassatt. Cassatt was the first important woman artist born in America, though she lived and worked in Paris when she grew up.

3. Based on a sculpture, *Little Dancer Aged Fourteen,* made by Edgar Degas between 1880 and 1881.

pages 20–21

POST-IMPRESSIONIST GALLERY

Post-Impressionist painters wanted even more freedom to express themselves than the Impressionists.

1. This picture, called *The Sleeping Gypsy* and painted in 1897, looks like a mysterious scene in some far-off desert. Yet the artist, Henri Rousseau, lived in the city of Paris. Rousseau liked painting wild animals—especially lions, tigers, and monkeys—and he often visited these animals at the zoo.

2. Based on Vincent van Gogh's painting from 1889, *The Starry Night.* Van Gogh worked hard to show his emotions in his art. Perhaps he wanted us to known from this painting how exciting it is to feel the wind and see bright stars light up the sky.

3. Based on the still-life painting, *Apples and a Pot of Primroses,* by Paul Cezanne, dated 1890–94. Cezanne arranged things very carefully to make a pleasing design of different shapes.

pages 22–23

TWENTIETH CENTURY, ABSTRACT GALLERY

Paintings don't have to show a recognizable person, place, or thing to be considered art. Artists sometimes use paintings and sculpture to express an idea or a feeling, or even to tell something about how they do their artwork.

1. Jackson Pollock made paintings like this one, *Portrait and a Dream,* dated 1953, not only by applying paint with a brush but also by pouring it right on the canvas. Some people call his work action painting. Can you see why?

2. Based on a 1921 cubist painting, *The Three Musicians,* by Pablo Picasso. Even though Picasso could draw realistic figures, he chose to depict these musicians by arranging shapes of different color paint.

3. Based on a mobile, *Lobster Trap and Fish Tail,* made by Alexander Calder in 1939. Mobiles are constructed to move with the slightest breeze.

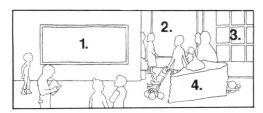

pages 24–25

**TWENTIETH CENTURY,
POP GALLERY**

In the 1960s, artists began using popular images from products, advertising, and the mass media as subjects for their artwork. These pop artists picture commonplace things about life, but show them to you in new and different ways. Since pop art is recent, all the artists whose work is represented in this gallery are still alive and busy doing their art.

1. Roy Lichtenstein painted *Whaam!* in 1963. He even decorates his own surroundings with pictures of everyday things: The elevator door to his work studio is painted to look like Swiss cheese!

2. Based on a 1966 painting, *Love,* by Robert Indiana

3. Based on Andy Warhol's painting, *Campbell's Soup Cans,* painted from 1961 to 1962

4. Based on a soft sculpture, *Floor Cake,* made in 1962 by Claus Oldenberg

TIPS FOR ENJOYING AN ART MUSEUM

- Take your time looking at art. You don't have to see everything on display in one visit.

- Take a break for lunch or some other activity after thirty or forty-five minutes. That way you won't get too tired.

- Wear comfortable shoes (like sneakers).

- Read the label posted near an art object when you want to know the title, artist, date made, and medium used.

- Touching the art is not permitted. Museums try to take care of valuable things and keep them from getting damaged, worn, or dirty.

- Ask at the information desk if there are materials or activities especially for children.

- Go on treasure hunts. Search paintings for things like hats, shoes, faces, hands; boys, girls; different animals. Whoever finds the most examples wins.

- Hunt for such features of art as circles, squares; shadows; certain colors; brushstrokes; different moods—like happy, sad, or mysterious.

- Hunt for sculptures that look smooth or rough.

- Make up stories about what is happening in different paintings. Try to predict what would happen if the picture continued to a next scene.

- Looking at portraits: Choose whom you would want to be your sister, brother, father, mother, or friend.

continued on page 32

- Be a detective. Try to figure out what job each person in the painting had, what kind of person each was, etc.
- Decide which artwork in a gallery you like best and which you like least. Explain why.
- Read books on art and artists. There are a number of good ones for children.

A *special thanks* to the people whose helpful advice we have used in this book:

Joyce Black, Linda Cohen, and Kathleen Walsh from the Art Institute of Chicago

Joan Cavanaugh from the Metropolitan Museum of Art, New York

Wendy Baring-Gould, Enid Gifford, and Sally Leahy from the Museum of Fine Arts, Boston

Lynn Russell from the National Gallery of Art, Washington, D.C.

DATE DUE